Aunt Fanny

The Big Nightcap Letters

Aunt Fanny

The Big Nightcap Letters

ISBN/EAN: 9783744700733

Printed in Europe, USA, Canada, Australia, Japan

Cover: Foto ©Andreas Hilbeck / pixelio.de

More available books at **www.hansebooks.com**

CARL RESCUING THE DOVE FROM THE HAWK

THE

BIG NIGHTCAP LETTERS;

BEING THE

FIFTH BOOK OF THE SERIES.

BY THE AUTHOR OF

THE SIX NIGHTCAP BOOKS, "AUNT FANNY'S STORIES,"

ETC., ETC.

NEW YORK:

D. APPLETON & COMPANY,

443 & 445 BROADWAY.

LONDON: 16 LITTLE BRITAIN.

1861.

TO

————, AND ————,

YOU know who;

THIS BOOK IS MOST LOVINGLY

𝔇𝔢𝔡𝔦𝔠𝔞𝔱𝔢𝔡.

PREFACE.

IT has always been my favorite theory, that the goodness and beauty of a truly Christian life in children could be taught quite as effectually by combining the gay with the grave, as by being altogether grave; for I chanced to remember that I invariably omitted all the latter portions of the story-books bestowed upon me when a child; and I have reason to believe that human nature is pretty much the same now as then.

In each of these little stories, it has been

my single aim to inculcate a desire in children to *do* good, to *be* good, and to seek prayerful assistance from the One source of all goodness—their Father in Heaven.

And now one word about the sixth book of this series. Trembling with a deep responsibility, I have ventured to write a fairy story, (that enchanted ground for the little ones,) through the whole of which I trust this thread of my theory has run *unbroken*. It is the last of our little friend, Lame Charley; and if the dear children who have made his Nightcaps theirs, will bear him, and me for his sake, in affectionate remembrance, it will gladden the heart of their loving

AUNT FANNY.

CONTENTS.

*** The stories written for the SEVEN NIGHT-
CAP CHILDREN remaining, will be found in " Little
Nightcap Letters."

BIG NIGHTCAP LETTERS.

THE FIRST LETTER.

INTRODUCTION.

ONE evening, when all the children, after the usual frolic with Crocus the cat and the TREMENDOUS DOG, had settled themselves for their "nightcaps," (their meaning of which word, of course, you all know,) the little mother cleared her throat, and paused, for she was feeling for a letter that was in her pocket.

"Something particularly good is coming to-night," whispered George to Anna.

"What makes you think so?"

"Don't you see how bright her eyes are? See! now she is hugging Charley, and kissing him;" and unable to resist this loving exhibition, he rushed from his seat to hug and kiss Charley, too, and ask him if he felt quite comfortable.

Charley thanked him with a loving look, and George went back to his seat, all in a glow.

"Children," said the little mother, "I received to-day a letter from Aunt Fanny! She says you have given her so many delightful stories, she thinks it is quite time to give you some in return."

THE FRIGHTENED OLD BACHELOR.

"Did you ever!" exclaimed the children, eagerly. "What a perfect bird of an Aunt Fanny! How perfectly delightful!"

"She wishes me to ask how you would like her to send you each a story, that you would know had been written especially for you?"

"Oh! oh! oh! what a capital idea!" cried all the children, clapping their hands at such a rate, that an old bachelor opposite opened the window and looked out with a spy-glass, to see where the fire was; and nearly frightened a lamplighter into fits, who was just at that very moment lighting a lamp at his door.

This most delightful announcement made the children chatter so fast, that Charley became nearly sick, laughing at what they said; for George again called Aunt Fanny a "perfect bird!" and Harry improved it by exclaiming that she was a perfect *cat* bird! which, of course, meant something very complimentary.

"Won't she write stories like a *mice!*" cried Johnny.

"And won't mamma read the writing like a precious kitten!" said Clara.

"Well, I never knew kittens could read writing before," laughed Harry.

"But, mamma," said Anna, "the letter looks very thick; is the first story in it?"

"Yes," said the little mother. "I will read what Aunt Fanny says—she says—

"And now, dear children, what do you

think? Do you remember the story of the 'Doctor' in the first Nightcap book? Well, that very doctor is now a young lady; and she has written a story on purpose for our dear little Charley. I think it is very charming; and I have sent it for the very first one, because I well know this will best please his loving brothers and sisters. Sarah, (the *real* name of the 'doctor,' you know,) has tried to write what would most gratify Charley's sweet and tender nature." Here the little mother stopped, and kissed her lame boy, and the children murmured, "dear, dear Charley." Then she read on—

"You will perceive that Sarah has endeavored to imitate the beautiful German style. Here is her story. Give Charley a kiss for us both before you begin."

And in almost breathless silence the mother read the title—

"THE LITTLE WHITE ANGEL.

"Some children stood in a group before the door of the village school-house one lovely summer evening.

"They were all talking pleasantly together, from Kline, the son of the rich and proud Hoffmeister, to little blue-eyed Carl, the only child of the poor baker.

"It is very true that Kline wore a velvet jacket, richly embroidered, while Carl's coat was old, and his wooden shoes were rough enough, in all conscience; but what of that? If they were good friends, what difference did *that* make, I should like to know? Wait till children become grown people, for pity's sake, before you expect them to measure each other's worth by what they possess or wear!

" 'The new schoolmaster, Meinherr Friedrich, comes to-morrow,' said Otto. 'I am so glad. I was weary of that old Master Hoffman, with his crooked problems and hard lessons.'

" 'So was I, truly,' cried Kline, who, although a good merry boy, hated his books as he did medicine.

" 'Ah, thou didst always like play better than work, my Kline,' said Max, ' and so do I. Meinherr Friedrich will be wise if he keep me and thee apart during school hours;

but come, see which can get home first—one, two, three!' and away they all scampered, laughing and shouting as only schoolboys can.

"The following day, the boys were all standing around the schoolhouse, when the door opened, and Master Friedrich himself, appeared, and cried in a cheery, hearty voice, 'Welcome, my children.'

"'Welcome, master,' cried they.

"And now they entered and took their seats, and were quite still while the good master read a short chapter in the Book of Books; and then reverently kneeling, prayed that the dear Jesus would guide him in his teachings, and bless them, and send His Holy Spirit to watch over them all.

" School began; the thumb-worn books were brought out—the lazy boys began to sigh and frown, and wish impatiently for the recess, and wonder why Latin dictionaries were ever invented; when, as if by magic, they found themselves listening to the pleasant voice of Master Friedrich, and actually understanding their lessons, so clear and simple were his explanations; and the time for recess came, to their great astonishment, long before they had expected.

" When the studies were over, the master drew from his desk a box; and whilst the children gathered around, he opened it and drew out charming little pink-and-white seashells, pretty pictures, and many other beau-

2

tiful things, which he gave to the children, with loving words.

"But the most lovely thing of all, was a little porcelain statuette of an angel. She stood, so fair, so pure—with her small white hands folded upon her breast, and her eyes uplifted, that the children gazed enchanted.

"'Oh the dear angel! the beautiful angel!' cried they all. 'Wilt thou not give it to me, Master Friedrich?'

"But the good master smiled, and said— 'The little angel is too lovely to be given to any boy who is not good and true of heart. We shall presently see who shall deserve her. He who brings me, to-morrow, the brightest thing on earth, shall have the angel.'

"At this the children looked at each

other, as if wondering what the good master might mean; but he said no more, and they went home thoughtful.

"The next day, after the lessons (which had now become so pleasant) were finished, the children clustered around the master to show him what they had brought.

"Some of the smaller ones had picked up sparkling stones on the road, and as they held them in the sunlight, were sure they must be something bright and precious.

"Some had polished up a shilling, until it shone like a little crown. Heinrich brought a watch-crystal, which his father had given him, and which he considered a wonder of transparent brightness; and Kline, the rich Hoffmeister's son, had brought a

paste buckle, made to imitate diamonds, than
which, in his opinion, nothing could be
brighter.

"All these things were laid on the schoolmaster's desk, side by side. The shillings
shone away famously, the pebbles and watch-
crystal did their best, but Kline's buckle
was the bravest of all.

"'Ah! mine's the brightest!' shouted
Kline, clapping his hands.

"'But where is little Carl?' said Master
Friedrich. 'He ran out just now.'

"All eyes were turned to the door, when
presently, in rushed Carl, breathless. In his
hands, held up lovingly against his neck,
was a poor little snow-white dove. Some
crimson drops upon the downy breast, showed that it was wounded.

"'Oh! master!' cried Carl, 'I was looking for something bright, when I came upon this poor little white dove. A cruel hawk had wounded it, and I caught it quickly, and ran here. Oh! I fear it will die!'

"Even as he spoke, the dove's soft eyes grew filmy; it nestled closer in Carl's neck, gave a faint cry, and died.

"Carl sank on his knees beside the master's desk, and from his eyes there fell upon the white dove's poor broken wing, two tears, large and bright.

"The master took the poor dead dove from his hands, and laid it tenderly down on the desk with the bright things; then raising Carl, he softly said—

"'My children, there is no brighter gem on earth, than a *tender, pitying tear.*'

"The boys were silent for a moment, for they felt that the master had decided that Carl had rightly won the angel, and then Kline cried out—

"'Nay, master, thou didst not fairly explain to us. I pray thee give us yet another trial.'

"'Yes, dear master,' said Max 'give us one more trial.'

"'What sayest thou Carl?' said Master Friedrich.

"'Yes, dear master,' answered the generous boy.

"The good master smiled thoughtfully, and his eyes rested for a moment, lovingly, upon Carl; then glancing round, he said— 'He who brings me the loveliest thing on earth to-morrow, shall have the angel.'

"The children clapped their hands, and departed satisfied.

"After school, the next day, Kline was the first to run up to Master Friedrich, and lay upon his desk what he considered the loveliest thing in the whole world—his new soldier cap, with the long scarlet feather, and bright golden tassel. Max came next, and placed beside the cap a small silver watch, his last birthday gift, with a bright steel chain attached. Otto brought a great picture-book, just sent him by his godmother; Rudolph a tiny marble vase, richly sculptured; and so on, until a still more motley collection than before lay upon Master Friedrich's desk.

"Then little Carl stepped modestly up,

and placed in the master's hand a pure white lily. The rich perfume filled the room; and bending over the flower, and inhaling the delicious fragrance, the master softly said— ' My children, the blessed Word of God says —Consider the lilies of the field, how they grow; they toil not, neither do they spin, and yet I say unto you, that even Solomon in all his glory was not arrayed like one of these. Carl has rightly chosen.'

"But murmurs arose; the children were not satisfied; and again they asked for another trial. And as before, good Master Friedrich inquired—

" ' What sayest thou, Carl?' and he answered as before, with generous haste, ' Yes, dear master.'

" 'Now this is the last time,' said the master. 'He who brings me the *best* thing on earth shall have the angel.'

" 'The very best thing on earth is plum cake!' cried Kline, on the third day, as he walked up to the desk, bearing a large cake, richly frosted, with a wreath of sugar roses round the edge. This he placed triumphantly before the master, sure of the prize.

" 'Nay, thou art wrong this time, Kline,' said Max. 'I asked my father what was the very best thing on earth, and he laughed, and gave me this golden guilder; the prize is mine.'

" 'Ah! but *my* father said that the very best was a good glass of Rhenish wine,' cried Otto, 'and I have brought a bottle of it thirty years old ; the prize is surely mine.'

"So they went on till all had placed their offering before the master.

"'And thou, Carl?' said he. 'What hast thou brought which thou thinkest the best on earth?'

"A crimson flush rose to the little boy's forehead, and coming softly forward, he took from his breast a *small, worn Testament*, pressed it to his lips, and then reverently laid it down with the rest" as he said, in a sweet, low voice—

"'My mother, dear master, says that God's precious Testament is far before all other possessions.'

"''Tis thine, my Carl!' cried the master,

snatching the boy to his breast. 'The white angel is thine! for there is nothing in the wide, wide world half so precious as the blessed words of Jesus;' and he placed the angel in the hands of the trembling boy.

"Kline knit his brows, and gazed with anger and disappointment at the little Carl; and the rest, seeing him do this, felt themselves aggrieved; but suddenly the cloud cleared from Kline's face, and rushing forward, he caught Carl in his arms, crying— 'Forgive me, dear Carl! now I am right glad thou hast won the prize!'

"Ah! the blessed effect of a bright example! Quickly joining hands, the children danced joyfully around the little Carl, who stood in the midst, the white angel pressed to his breast, his fair hair falling in curls on his shoulders, and his blue eyes full of holy tears.

"The good Master Friedrich also wept for joy, and prayed, from the depth of his pure and simple heart, that Jesus would bless this lesson to the children's everlasting good. He had turned away that none might perceive his tears.

"But One in heaven saw them, Master Friedrich."

The story was finished, but no one spoke, for the tears were softly falling from Charley's eyes; and the rest of the children, with quivering lips, were gazing in his face. At last he said, in a low voice—"What a lovely story! and how sweet and good little Carl was! Dear mamma! we will all try to be generous and good, as he was; and we all know what a precious book the Bible is. I love Carl; and I thank Aunt Fanny and Miss Sarah with all my heart, for writing this beautiful story about him."

And now all the children, with subdued and tender glances, kissed their dear mother and Charley, and went quietly to bed, thinking of the dear little Carl, and wishing softly to each other, that their mother had thought of asking *them* to find the "brightest and loveliest and best thing on earth," for they hoped they should have done just as the dear Carl did.

THE SECOND LETTER.

For Harry.

DEAR HARRY:—I have happened upon an odd story of a heedless namesake of yours, and as you are a dear head-over-heels little fellow, I think you will be both amused and instructed by reading it; or at any rate, you will resolve never to cut any thing like the very extraordinary capers the other Harry did, either in the vegetable or travelling line. Once, when you were a very little fellow and were visiting at a cousin's house in the country, you busied yourself all one morning, pulling up radishes, eating the roots, and then setting the tops back in the earth, and when the gardener came to gather some for tea, he found them all wilted and flat to the ground. Do you remember how you had to run for it, when he caught sight of you laughing at him? and how his having the rheumatism in his knee, so that he could not move fast, was all that saved you from a good thrashing? *I* do. So here is the story, and hoping it will be very serviceable in helping you to "mend your ways," I am your loving

AUNT FANNY.

"HEEDLESS HARRY.

"'Oh! how I do hate to write exercises!' exclaimed Harry, one Monday afternoon in the summer time; 'what's the use? they are abominable!' and he stamped his foot and threw down his pen, clapped his hat on his head, and rushed out of the front door.

"No wonder he was called 'heedless' Harry; for he was so thoughtless, that he never stopped one moment to reflect, when he set about doing any thing, whether or not it would get him into trouble; and consequently he was always in some scrape or other. He was old enough, certainly, to know better, and pleasant enough, in other respects, to be liked very much by all who

knew him. He was full of fun, perfectly
fearless, and bore an accidental scratch or
tumble like a man. But, dear me! what a
heedless, careless little scamp! That very
morning, before school began, his mother had
sent him into the garden to gather vegetables. He cut the carrots so that they would
stand up on end, and with great onions began knocking them down, as if they were
tenpins; then he had a game of jack-straws
with some small slender beans, and ended
the vegetable business by stringing a dozen
red peppers and tying them round the cat's
neck, making her sneeze her head nearly off;
for the poor thing went 'tchitz! tchitz!
tchitz!' for a quarter of an hour.

"When he was tired of laughing at her, he

3

marched away to skip stones in the brook, and ended by slipping on the bank and tumbling into the water, and treating himself to a very thorough ducking.

"Harry lived with his parents on a large pleasant farm, about twenty miles from the city of New York. He had never been in New York; and this afternoon, at which my story commences, when he rushed to the front door, he put his hand in his pockets and said to himself: 'I've a great mind to run away! I know I shall catch it to-morrow, about that old exercise, and I can't write it. I won't! now!'

"He walked to the fence, and climbing up, looked over into a neighbor's meadow.

"A beautiful white horse was quietly grazing, and lazily switching the flies off his back with his long and silken tail.

"'Halloo!' exclaimed heedless Harry, 'there's Lightfoot! Jolly! what a chance to go off on my travels! I'll catch him. There! now he is drinking out of the brook. I'll go and jump on his back.'

"As usual, the little scapegrace had entirely forgotten that the horse was very swift and spirited, and also that he did not belong to him or his parents. So Harry, with one bound, jumped the fence, paying no kind of attention to a great thorn which tore down the leg of his pantaloons for half a yard, ran up to Lightfoot, caught him with one hand by his flowing mane, placed the other on his back, and tried to mount him.

"Horses are animals, but they are not stupid or fools for all that. So Lightfoot, while he kept his nose in the brook, had been quietly watching Harry out of the corner of his eye; and when the young gentleman tried to jump on his back, the horse gave a quick little start to one side, and a knowing flourish with his tail, which sent Mr. Harry plump into the brook for the second time that day, and then Lightfoot scampered off with a neigh which sounded remarkably like a horse laugh.

"The angry boy scrambled up the low bank like a lame grasshopper, and screamed out, 'You hateful old thing! I *will* get on your back! see if I don't!' So he cut a stout branch from a tree, stripped it, made it whistle through the air, and with a spiteful chuckle advanced once more upon Lightfoot.

"The horse gave another neigh. Harry approached him softly, hiding the whip behind him, smoothed his neck, and patted his side, and then, with a sudden spring, leaped upon his back.

"Lightfoot stood perfectly still. Then Harry clucked his tongue against his palate to coax him to go.

"But the horse pretended not to hear him. 'Get up! Get up!' cried Harry. 'Come now, get up, I tell you.'

"Lightfoot went on eating, as if there was nobody within a mile of him.

"Harry became more and more impatient; he thumped the horse with his knees, and drummed with his heels, and finding that did no good, he raised the switch to strike him.

"Lightfoot was a 'cute' Yankee horse, he wasn't 'raised' in Vermont for nothing; so when he caught sight of the switch, he ducked his head, and off went Harry like a flash of lightning, and found himself sprawling on the grass.

"You would think that was enough; and that Harry, after all these gymnastics, would go home like a boy that had some sense pounded into him by all these hard knocks. Not at all. Up he sprang, ran to Lightfoot, and jumped for the third time upon his back.

"'Get up! Get up! you goose!' he cried. This time the horse heard him, without any doubt; he gave a flourish with his long tail, cleared the fence with a bound, and rushed down the road like an arrow shot from a bow.

"And now our young friend would gladly have dismounted, but that was easier thought of than done. To get off a horse in full gallop may not be difficult, if you are not particular whether you come down on your heels or your head. Harry reflected, that though possibly his head might be harder than the stones in the road, and the stones would be hurt the most, yet there was rather a chance that the stones might crack his head instead, so he concluded to hold on if he could.

"On dashed Lightfoot for miles and miles, with Harry clinging for dear life to his neck and mane. At last they approached a large town, and Lightfoot stopped of his own accord at a public house.

"Out came the landlord, staring with surprise, and lifted Harry off, half-dead with fatigue and fright, while the hostler led the horse to the stable.

"After the heedless boy had washed his face and brushed his clothes, he felt better, but desperately hungry; there was no fun in that; so he concluded to hunt up a dinner.

"When he entered the dining-room, the people looked at him from head to foot. Of course this was because they were admiring him, he thought; so he drew himself up, and putting on an air of dignity, as if he was a gentleman on his travels, he said: 'I want my dinner. Bring me a beefsteak, some potatoes, and an apple-dumpling.'

" At these words the landlord advanced, put his hand on Harry's shoulder, and said: 'Who are you?'

" Harry preferred eating to talking just then, so he answered: 'Give me a beefsteak directly. When I have eaten my dinner I will tell you my history.'

" 'Um! we'll see—tell it to me this instant, or you may get your dinner as you can, like a gipsy under a fence—but you won't have any here.'

" 'I will have it,' cried Harry, in a rage.

" 'You shan't!' said the landlord.

" 'I will!' cried Harry.

" 'John,' said the landlord to the waiter, 'I forbid your bringing any dinner to this impertinent little scamp.'

" ' Impertinent yourself! ' screamed Harry, nearly beside himself with passion ; and he seized a glass to throw it in the landlord's face.

" At this riotous noise, some more servants and the landlady rushed into the room; and the latter screaming out, ' You little wretch ! ' and snatching up a broomstick, rushed full tilt at Harry, who, concluding that it was best not to wait for the fight, jumped over the table, darted out of the door, and flew up the street.

" He ran for a long time, as if a mad dog were after him, until he had gained the outskirts of the town, and stopping, breathless and exhausted, began to reflect upon his situation.

" We always make remarkably wise re-
flections when we are suffering from our misconduct. Harry began to think he had been
acting very like a donkey, and would very
willingly have returned home, and taken to
studying his hated lessons.

" Night was now approaching; the twi-
light deepened and darkened; and it was
only by the stars which came peeping out
one by one, that he could see his way. A
strange feeling of dread and loneliness came
over him, and he was rejoiced at last to see
dimly before him a large barn. Jumping
the fence, he went up and tried the door;
fortunately it was open, and our heedless
friend was glad enough to throw himself
down on a heap of fragrant hay, and spite

of his hunger, was soon in a dreamless sleep.

"The dismal screech (for it isn't crowing) of one of those long-legged Shanghai roosters, awoke him just as the dawn was streaking the sky; and shaking the hay from his dress, Harry went out into the road again.

"He was walking along, wondering whether he should ever see home again. A market-wagon came up behind him, and he turned to inquire his way.

"'Where do you come from?' said the market man. Harry told him. 'Bless my wig!' said the man, 'you can't get home to-day, no how you can fix it. Come with me. I'm going to York to sell my sass, and to-morrow I will take you half-way home.'

"' Jolly ! that's a good fellow,' cried Harry, brightening up, 'and you'll be a better fellow yet, if you'll give me one of these rosy-cheeked apples; I'm hungry enough to swallow the horse and wagon.'

"' Massy sakes! air you? Well, eat one out each basket. 'Twon't make any difference; they don't count apples.'

"So the heedless boy went into the apple-eating business with all his teeth; and before he had made a finish of it, they had crossed the Jersey City ferry, and rumbled into the streets leading to Washington Market, where the market man speedily disposed of his fruit and vegetables, which he called 'sass.' When he had concluded this business, he took Harry down into one of the cellars, where he ordered a nice breakfast, and strange to say, Harry had some inside room left, for he did his part in clearing the plates in fine style.

" After that, they went to a public house, where the good market man left Harry, as he had some business in a distant part of the city; but he charged the boy on no account to leave the house till he returned. Harry promised he would not.

" When he was gone, Harry put his nose out of the window. The day was clear and beautiful, and at the end of the street he could see the water.

" 'Dear me,' said Harry to himself, 'what's the harm of going to look at the water. It's a real ocean. I've never seen the ocean. I'll just take one peep and come back.'

" Down he went to the edge of the pier, and sat upon the end, to stare around him. A steamboat coming quickly alongside, one of the waves she made flew up in Harry's face, and splashed him from top to toe. He jumped up in such a particular hurry, that a sailor on a large ship on the other side, burst out laughing, saying, ' Are you afraid, Mr. Sugar Candy ? '

" ' Afraid ! I ! ' cried Harry, indignantly, and turning round suddenly, his foot tripped against a stone, and he tumbled over backwards into the water.

" Harry opened his mouth to bawl, but instead of that, had it well filled with salt water. The sailor ran faster than a lamplighter, jumped in the water, caught Harry by the collar, and dragged him on shore, and set him down in the sun to dry.

"While Harry was drying, the sailor asked him all manner of questions, and soon had his whole history. Then the cunning fellow invited him to dinner; and heedless Harry, delighted to get on board a great ship, went with him, never thinking again of the kind, generous market man.

"And now, boys, and girls too, read for your benefit what happened next. The old sailor was commissioned to find one or two cabin boys for his ship, which sailed that very evening, as soon as the tide served. Harry was strong and quick—Harry was fearless—Harry had run away from home— Harry wanted to see the world—Harry was the boy, the very dandy, for a cabin boy; so

the sailor proposed that Harry should continue his travels in his company.

" ' Where are you going ? ' said our young
friend.

" ' To Senegal,' said the sailor.

" ' And what sort of a place is Senegal ? '

" ' Senegal,' answered the sailor, ' is a
most magnificent country, where the rivers
are made of milk, and the mountains of sugar.
The rain is composed of lemonade, and the
birds fall down from the trees all stuffed and
roasted, ready to eat, from morning till night.
The trees are covered with sugar-plums ; and
all the streams are full of goldfishes, which
come when you whistle to them. They are
real gold, and used for money by the inhabit-
ants ! '

4

"'But — do they ever _write exercises there?_' asked Harry, with a cunning twinkle in his eye.

"'NEVER!' cried the sailor, who saw what the trouble was with the silly boy. 'The king of this delightful country has expressly forbidden it. He has burned down all the colleges and blown up all the schools.'

"'Jolly!' cried Harry, snapping his fingers, 'that's the country for me! I'll go with you, sure pop!'

"You perceive that heedless Harry did not use very elegant language, but as a true historian, I must tell you of persons, places, and things just as they are, and I hope your good sense will teach you to avoid all such vulgarities.

" The sailor, taking advantage at once of Harry's delight in his account of Senegal, carried him to the captain, and making an awkward bow, said : ' Captain, here is a new hand.'

" ' Good ! ' cried the captain. ' He looks strong. I hope he won't die of weariness and fatigue, like the other ones.'

" At these words, Harry began to feel rather uncomfortable. ' What ! ' said he to the sailor, as they left the cabin, ' do boys have to work on board your ship ? '

" ' Sartain, for sure ; all the time,' said the sailor, laughing.

" ' I want to go away,' cried Harry, already disgusted with the maritime service.

" ' What's that you say ? ' shouted the

sailòr, with a mocking air. 'You forget, my fine friend, that I gave you a dinner; pay me for it.'

"Harry shook his pockets, they were empty. 'If you can't pay, you must stay,' cried the sailor, and just then the ship left the harbor.

"The heedless boy burst into tears. Alas! sorrow and repentance came too late! It was only now that he remembered his father and mother, probably made ill with grief at his disappearance; and the worry the good market man must be in, thinking the boy to whom he had been so kind was lost, perhaps murdered, in the great and wicked city.

"In the midst of these doleful lamentations, the sailor came up and pulled Harry by the ear.

" ' Come, you sniffling booby! go to work,' he said.

" Harry looked at him in astonishment.

" ' My eyes! do you think you can eat and drink for nothing? Come, take this broom; do you hear?'

" Our dismal friend took the broom, and would liked to have broken it over the head of the brutal sailor, but he was not strong enough.

" ' Will you go to sweeping or not?' cried the sailor, swearing in the most terrible manner.

" ' I don't want to sweep,' said Harry.

" ' Don't want to?'

"'No!' Harry, perfectly red with anger, threw down the broom, and crossed his arms.

"'Oh! that's the way you behave, is it?' said the sailor. 'Come to me, Susan.'

"With that he caught up a knotted rope's end, and gave Harry half a dozen blows over his shoulders. You see blows from Susan were given rather more frequently on board ship than sugar plums. 'Now, my dear friend,' said the sailor, 'this is only the beginning of your fun. Now, you know what will happen if you are idle. Susan is my wife, and my name is Jack Bowsprit; so take care of Susan and Jack, and pick up the broom and sweep the deck, if you don't want some more of our delicate attentions.'

"Poor Harry began to sweep with a trembling lip, his heart swelling with rage and misery: then he had to wash the decks, and after that to scrape the carrots and peel the potatoes, and then he was rewarded by having a piece of salt pork given him for his supper, and eating it with the sailors.

"Harry was in despair. When supper was over he came up and sat on the deck to think. Tears came thick and fast as his misconduct and its miserable consequences rose up in his mind. He knelt down for the first time since he had left home, and prayed his Heavenly Father to forgive him, and promised that if he only was permitted to see his dear parents again, he would indeed be an obedient, thoughtful boy: he would try to be so from that moment.

"Meanwhile, a fair, keen breeze rose, and continued for many days, and the ship sailed swiftly on to her destination. In a month more they beheld Senegal. Entering the river, they soon came to Saint Louis, where they landed.

"You can imagine how rejoiced Harry was to set foot once more upon the firm earth—not with the permission of the captain, though: for fearing they might keep him on the ship all the time, in the dusk of the evening he slid down a rope that was hanging over the side, and, scrambling on shore without being seen, made the best possible use of his heels.

"Liberty is a very fine thing; but some other things are wanted besides to make it perfect—dinner, for instance, and a house containing a comfortable bed to sleep in.

" Harry was not much afraid at first at finding himself in a savage country, alone and unprotected. To the heedless, whatever is new is charming.

" It was now bright moonlight, serene and still. Harry, exhausted and tired with his flight, lay down on the luxuriant grass.

" At home, lying down in such a bed would have given him so severe a cold in his head, that he would have nearly sneezed and snuffled it off. Not so in Senegal. Still there were other inconveniences, for Harry had not rested for five minutes, when he heard a stealthy footstep; his heart began to beat. He had learned in his Geography that Senegal was full of wild beasts, as well as the sugar plums the treacherous sailor talked about. He began to wish he had staid in the ship; but if he returned, there was Jack Bowsprit, and there was SUSAN as sure as a gun. It is no doubt very disagreeable to be devoured by wild beasts; but then again it is very painful to be beaten by a Susan. Harry was sure of the beating if he returned, and he was not quite sure of being eaten up if he remained; so he concluded to stay.

"While he was cogitating all these things, he heard again the same stealthy tread; and, in a moment, he saw in the bright moonlight a jackal, about the size of a big dog.

"Our heedless Harry was without wea-

pons of defence, but he was by no means
without courage. Up he sprang, seized a
large stone, and flung it at the jackal; at almost the same instant the wild beast leaped
at him and bit his leg.

"Both gave a howl of pain at the same
moment. Happily, Harry was not much
hurt; while the jackal, with another cry,
lay dead at his feet.

"Harry gazed at his fallen enemy, his
heart beating with excitement; he could
not help thinking that if any thing a quarter
as bad had happened to him at home, his
kind mother could not have found caresses
and court-plaster enough to console him;
and here he was, alone, and wounded. He
went to a stream near by, and washed and

tied up his leg as well as he could; and then
he began to think how he could pass the
night without danger. To rest on the bosom
of the earth was not safe; another jackal
might come after the first to help him pick
the bones. To be sure he might regain the
ship—but SUSAN!! At last he concluded
he would leave the earth, and climb a tree.
After much toil, and terrible scratching and
scrambling, he managed to get into an immense tree, and settling himself in a fork
like an arm-chair, he fell into a troubled
sleep.

"The first rays of the sun awoke our
hero. Just as he was about to descend from
the tree, he heard a slight noise above. He
looked up, and there he saw (oh! oh! what

THE ANACONDA THAT HARRY KILLED.

I hope you may never see except in a Menagerie or Barnum's Museum) an enormous boa constrictor, at least fifty feet long, suspended from the top boughs of the tree, twisting about. With a fierce and horrible hiss, which froze the blood in Harry's veins, he twisted, and turned, and looked at the terrified boy.

"Harry screamed aloud. He had read of this dreadful monster, how he thought nothing of swallowing a bull whole for his breakfast; and, of course, our young friend would be only a side dish—a mere trifle. The boa advanced towards him with another dreadful hiss, which seemed to say—'Here's a nice little mouthful! wait for me.'

"But Harry was determined to make

one desperate attempt to postpone the feast. He slid down the trunk of the tree like lightning, and when he stood on the ground he did not stop to ascertain which way the wind blew, but ran like a rail car, under full steam, panting and screaming very much as they do.

"All at once he stopped short, for a terrible roaring, like an immense peal of thunder, shook the earth. What was it? Oh, mercy! it was a great lion who was just waking up.

"What was the luckless, heedless boy to do? Between the lion and the boa constrictor, Harry was certainly lost. Whichever was to eat him, it was certain he would make a breakfast for one of them; for on turning

THE LION.

his head, he saw, to his increased horror, that the monstrous snake had followed him; and at the same moment an enormous lion appeared running, making bounds as high as the arch of a bridge.

"Harry threw himself on his knees. For one moment he was a prey to the most agonizing despair. Then he clasped his hands together, and implored for pardon for all his faults; and then rising, with a white and terror-stricken face, he endeavored to await with fortitude the coming of his cruel fate.

"But now a very remarkable thing happened. Harry, nearly petrified with amazement, saw the lion and boa advance with savage fierceness upon each other!

"Oh! then he thanked God in his heart!

He carefully crept to one side, and watched, with an eagle-like glance, what would happen next.

"With a wild roar and savage bound, the lion sprang upon the serpent, and tried to tear him in pieces, while the boa, hissing like a thousand geese, twisted himself, fold after fold, round the body of his enemy, crushing him, squeezing him, and rolling over till his bones cracked. The angry roar changed into a cry of despair and frenzy. Soon that cry became weaker and weaker, fainter and fainter, then ceased altogether—the lion was dead.

"The monstrous serpent, without waiting to lay the table, or call for mustard, licked his prey all over, and then swallowed him whole.

"You will ask, perhaps, why Harry did not run away. He had two excellent reasons. The first was, he did not know where in this part of the world to run; he might find a tiger at the very next turn; and the second, that he was too frightened to move.

"So Harry stood by and witnessed this ruthless, shocking spectacle, to the end, his heart beating as if it would leap out of his breast; and when the boa had finished his frightful meal, the poor little fellow observed that the monster was so gorged, he could scarcely move, and that in a few moments more he was fast asleep.

"'There is one good thing,' he said to himself, 'the awful thing don't care to breakfast twice, so I am safe for the present.'

5

"As the boa seemed perfectly helpless, he conceived a splendid but bold idea, for he was by no means a timid child.

"He approached and stamped upon the tail of the reptile, who remained immovable; then he made a cord of a vine that was growing near, with a running knot at the end, and slipping this round the boa's neck, and drawing it with all his might, he strangled the serpent.

"Hardly had he concluded this brilliant achievement, when he heard the galloping of horses. Terrified and trembling, he waited half in hope and half in fear for what was to come, when in a few moments, to his great joy, he beheld some officers of the marine service, whom he was sure were Americans, approaching him.

" What was their astonishment at seeing a little boy standing, pale, and with eyes wild and distended with excitement, over the dead body of an enormous snake.

" ' Good gracious ! ' exclaimed the one who appeared to be the captain, ' what on earth are you doing with that amiable creature ? '

" Harry, with his eyes full of tears, simply told his history.

" The officers were very much affected. They belonged to an American ship of war that was just about returning home.

" ' Would you like to go back with us ? ' said the captain, kindly.

" ' Oh, Captain ! ' cried Harry, ' gladly will I go with you, but—'

" ' But what ? ' asked the captain.

" ' I want you to promise me that I shan't be beaten by Susan.'

" ' What on earth do you mean ? ' cried the captain, as he and the rest burst into a laugh.

" Harry explained how Jack Bowsprit used to beat him with a rope's end, which he called his wife, Susan, and how he hated Susan worse than poison.

" They all laughed again at this, and the captain promised that Susan should be thrown overboard as far as he was concerned, and that he should be taken safely home.

" So Harry went with the officers, who treated him as if he was their son; and after a prosperous voyage, he arrived safely at

New York; and money was given him to get home.

"That very evening Harry stood once more before his sorrowing, almost broken-hearted parents. What did they do? They did not utter one word of reproach; they just opened their arms, and the boy flung himself upon their breasts; and amid tears and blessings all was forgiven. But not forgotten. Oh, no! for Harry, once so heedless, tried his utmost to correct his faults, and with God's help, he *succeeded;* and now he is so steady, industrious, and obedient, that it is almost impossible to believe that he ever was called

HEEDLESS HARRY."

There was many a roguish, laughing

look cast at Harry as this strange story was being read; and when it was finished, George exclaimed, eagerly—"Oh, mamma! what a pity Aunt Fanny did not know about Harry, and the old black cook, and the dishcloth! Wouldn't she have laughed?"

"Tell us about it, Harry, do! do!" cried all the brothers and sisters.

The children knew the story as well as Harry, but they delighted to watch the sparkle of his eyes, and his animated gestures, for to tell the truth, he *did* enjoy mischief beyond words to describe.

"Well," cried Harry, jumping up, "you see I *would* go down in the kitchen and teaze the cook; and she could never touch me with the broomstick, because I ran full tilt;

and she was very fat, you know, always trod on her dress, and sometimes came down flat on her nose.

"Well, one day she said—'If you come in the kitchen again, I'll pin the dishcloth fast to your jacket!' I *came right back.* 'PIN IT!' said I, 'that's all I want.' So she pinned it, and I stood very, *very* still till it was done. Then I made one jump in the air, and gave one tremendous shout, and put *square* up stairs for mother's room, the cook after me; but I ran fastest, she was so fat. I got in the room first, tore off the dishcloth —her best dishcloth—bran new, and threw it into the very middle of the fire; and she had the pleasure of seeing the last of her new dishcloth blazing up the chimney. So that's what a cook gets when she pins her dish-cloth on a boy."

The children clapped their hands, and screamed with laughter at this story; and they laughed still harder, when Harry put on a comical, half-provoked look, and added, " But you know mother made me take the very money I was going to buy a new ball with, and buy a yard of crash to make another dishcloth for the cook; that crashed *me*, so I don't think I shall burn any more for the present."

And now the children, bidding each other " good night," went skipping and dancing to bed, delighted with the evening's entertainment, wondering who would have the next story from Aunt Fanny.

THE THIRD LETTER.

POOR RICH LITTLE EVA.

For Anna.

DEAR ANNA:—I have lately been reading a book full of pure and beautiful thoughts, called "Vernon Grove," and the other evening I became acquainted with the authoress. She is a most lovely lady, dignified and graceful; and I had a very delightful conversation with her about books.

In Vernon Grove there is a short story

about a dear little girl, which story interested me so much, that I asked permission of the authoress to copy it out for you. Here it is, somewhat enlarged and altered, but the main parts just as she wrote it. I know, dear Anna, it is exactly such a tender, sweet story, as will most gratify your affectionate heart; so it is yours, with a kiss from your loving

AUNT FANNY.

"POOR RICH LITTLE EVA.

" On a curtained bed, in a darkened chamber in the city of Charleston, not many years ago, lay a beautiful lady, pale—almost dying; but, oh! how happy, for her earnest prayer had been answered, and God had at last given her the blessing of a child, and the little tender life was even now nestling soft as a rose-leaf in her bosom.

"It was late in the sweet spring-time, which in that southern country is so beautiful. A hushed and joyous stillness reigned in the house, but every lip was smiling, from the good old black cook, who was 'so grad missis ben got her heart's desire,' to the funny little fellow with his wool standing up in kinks all over his head, who ran of errands, and who evinced his delight by walking on his kinky head all about the yard.

"Never was baby more welcomed. A daughter, too, just what her parents desired —a darling girl to be a companion for her mother all day long.

"The nursery was now the most interesting and delightful room in the house. Though evidences of boundless wealth and exquisite taste were in every part, until the baby came, it was only a grand, silent, gloomy mansion; for no young pure voice had awakened the echoes in the stately halls—no little pattering feet made there delicious heart-music.

"But *now* what a magic change! How friends flocked to see the wonderful nursery which the expectant mother had been so happy in preparing; how they peeped into the bureau drawers, and admired the piles of rare lace and snowy lawn, which were to enfold the delicate limbs of this favored child.

"And then the surprising and splendid

toys in gold and silver! the beautiful pictures already hung upon the walls, painted by
skilful artists, telling stories that she would
understand almost from infancy, of 'Little
Red Riding Hood,' 'The Lamented Babes in
the Wood,' and 'Little Mary and her pretty
pet Lamb, who *would* go to school with her.'
Ah! what a beautiful world was to be opened
to the sight and mind of that sweet spring
flower.

"Every day the good doctor came to see
the mother and the little baby, and every
day the mother grew stronger; and the
greatest delight of both parents was to look
at their new child, and softly kiss its tender
cheek, and feel the velvet touch of its precious
little hands.

"Then, very soon, it grew so knowing, and showed such surprising quickness, far beyond (the *parents* thought) of any baby ever seen or read of since the beginning of the world. Of course it was very red at first, but then the red was such a beautiful shade. It hadn't the least speck of hair; but what of that? There was a lovely expression about even the *back* of its head; really quite intellectual.

"Very soon, it would start at an unexpected noise or touch, and if dinner did not come at the very moment it was wanted, little Eva (for that was her sweet name) could cry in a manner to astonish you; but then, such an excellent cry! so loud and strong, that it was certain she had splendid lungs.

And what more could a mother's heart desire? And her precious treasure was watched and guarded night and day by a mother's love, stronger than death.

"But what is this? The good doctor watches little Eva as she grows, and always when he looks at her, a sad, strange expression comes over his face; and one day, when going down stairs, he paused, and turned to go back, but did not, for he said aloud to himself: 'Not yet; they cannot bear it yet; and perhaps, after all, I may be in the wrong.'

"They were both so happy—that young father and mother! How they pitied all the poor married people who had no children!

"But the next day after this the good

doctor decided not to withhold the communication, whatever it might be, from Eva's father and mother. As soon as he entered the room, he said abruptly: 'Nurse, bring me the child.' He stood by a window, and threw wide open the darkened blinds. The little Eva was brought to him just from her morning toilette, fresh, sweet, and pure as a rain-brightened flower; her long embroidered dress sweeping the carpet, and soft lace nestling about her tiny arms.

" 'Oh, dear doctor!' exclaimed the young mother, ' do not take the baby there! That bright glare of light has dazzled even my strong eyes; and how can her feeble sight endure it?'

. " 'It is necessary, madam,' replied the

doctor. He seemed to be a cross old fellow, but beneath his gruff manner was hidden a great, kind heart.

"He took the child, and having sent the nurse away, turned from the mother, who lay anxiously watching him. He gazed fixedly at little Eva, while he exposed her beautiful and tender eyes to the bright glare of the morning sun. His brow was contracted into a great heavy frown, and a short but deep sigh escaped him; but he never took his eyes from her face: then he forced the lids, with their long silken fringes, far away from the ball of the eye, and little Eva was now screaming with the pain caused by this rough and cruel treatment. Alas! a deeper shade of anxiety crossed the doctor's face, and the hard and unfeeling man, as the weeping mother thought him, drew the infant tenderly to his breast, and murmured in a low tone, ' *Poor little thing! poor little helpless thing!*' and gave her back to her nurse, and went away without saying another word.

"That same evening the doctor came again. It was very unusual for him to come after dark, and his great creaking boots and rough manner would have broken in upon a very pretty group.

"But he went softly up stairs, and looked in the room, unseen himself. There was the happy mother wrapped in a cashmere, and half-buried in an immense arm-chair, with a sweet motherly look upon her face, watching her darling.

" Close to his wife, Eva's father sat, holding her in his arms; and, wonderful to tell, for a *man*, holding her quite comfortably; for he had lulled her to sleep with a lullaby of his own composition, the language of which was utterly unknown to the rest of the company. He was learning to talk 'baby talk,' and was really getting on very well, and just now he was looking extremely proud and happy at his success in soothing the little one.

" Opposite to these happy parents sat Mr. Vernon, a noble-looking gentleman, and his wife, a beautiful lady, uncle and aunt to the baby; and, in the distance, was the faithful black nurse, old Dinah, fast asleep, and quite as happy, in her own opinion, as the rest of the party.

" Presently the father laid the baby tenderly down in her beautiful cradle, and while gently rocking her, said softly : ' I wonder what the baby was thinking about while I sang to her ? '

" ' She looked so wonderfully wise,' said the mother.

" ' Did you ever come across that lovely little poem—" What is the little one thinking about ? "' said Mr. Vernon. ' I can only remember the last part of it, though my little daughter has often read it to me,' and he recited, in a sweet, low voice, this exquisite little fragment :

" What is the little one thinking about ?
    What does she think of her mother's eyes ?
    What does she think of her mother's hair ?

What, of the cradle roof that flies
Forward and backward through the air ?
What does she think of her mother's breast,
Round and beautiful, smooth and white,
Seeking it ever with fresh delight—
Cup of her life, and couch of her rest ?
What does she think, when her quick embrace
Presses her hand, and buries her face
Deep, where the heart-throbs sink and swell
With a tender love she can never tell,
  Though she murmurs the words
  Of all the birds,
Words she had learned to murmur well ?
Now she thinks she'll go to sleep !
I can see the shadow creep
Over her eyes in soft eclipse
Over her brow, and over her lips.
Out to her little finger-tips !
Softly sinking—down she goes !
Down—she—goes !—down—she—goes !
See ! she is hushed in sweet repose."

" As the doctor gazed on this lovely scene, and heard the beautifully touching words so fitly spoken, instead of smiling, he frowned and sighed, for his heart was troubled.

" Coming forward, he grumbled out, ' A family party, I see.'

" ' Yes,' said the father, rising and smiling; ' and no one but yourself would find a welcome.'

" ' So much the better,' growled the doctor. ' Nurse, light the gas.'

" ' We have not lit it yet,' said the young mother, pointing to the two wax lights in a distant corner, ' because they tell me the eyes of infants are very weak and tender.'

" The doctor took no notice of this, only nodded to the nurse; and she, standing in mortal fear that he would cut her head off immediately if she hesitated, obeyed his order.

"The mother looked at her little child, who was still peacefully sleeping, and then shaded her eyes with her hand from the sudden blaze of light, thinking that though the doctor seemed very cruel, he must be doing what was right.   Poor young mother!

"'I only need this last test before I tell you what it means,' said the doctor.   'Here, give me the child.'

"The father tenderly laid the little Eva in his arms, though quite at a loss to imagine what experiment was to be tried. The light was certainly too strong to be let suddenly into a darkened room, he thought; but the doctor knew best. It was strange that only the noble-looking gentleman, Mr. Vernon, seemed to divine the meaning of the rough but kind-hearted man, but he knew only too well; he was *sadly sure*. I will tell you why, presently.

"And now the tender head of the sleeping child lay helplessly against the physician's rough coat, encircled by his arm.

"Suddenly he dashed some cold water, that stood near, into her face.

"Little Eva awoke, and opened her dark blue eyes immediately under the bright stream of light. She did not cry; she did not shrink; calmly she looked up, never flinching, never winking as she lay.

"The doctor raised her nearer and nearer

to the flame; he turned the screws, and let out each burner to its fullest capacity, and passed his hands rapidly to and fro close to the child's eyes, then turning towards the wondering, panic-stricken group, who were slowly beginning to understand the meaning of that fearful pantomime, he laid her once more in her father's arms, and looking in his face, said, in a rough, broken voice, while a great tear trembled in his eye—'God help little Eva,—SHE IS BLIND.'

" The doctor went away that night with the sorrowful wail of the poor parents smiting his heart.

" He came again and again, but nevermore in that house did he open the door upon a group so smilingly happy, as that which greeted him on the fatal night, when he told them the dreadful truth, that their child would never see their faces, for she was blind.

"And now I will tell you about Mr. Vernon. When he was quite a young man, rich, handsome, and surrounded with friends, he was taken ill with a dreadful fever, which left him totally blind. For a long, long time he murmured at God's will, and refused to believe there was any thing left worth living for; but God's ways are not our ways, and in His own good time He so softened the wilful heart of the blind man, so that he became not only resigned, but happy.

"After a few years, God gave him a beautiful wife, who loved him more because

of the affliction which made him so depend-
ent upon her loving care; and oh! how I
hope that all who are reading this true story
will have a tender pity for those upon whom
God has caused outward darkness to fall.
They cannot see the sunshine, or the beautiful flowers—let them *feel* the warm sunshine
of a loving heart.

"In due course of time Mr. Vernon had
two lovely children, the elder a pretty little
maiden, with deep blue eyes, and dark, wavy
hair, whose sweet name was Ruth. The dear
little girl was six years old before the other
darling came to gladden his parents' heart,
and having no companions but her blind
father and gentle mother, she grew to be
quite a dignified little woman. None so

proud and happy as Ruth, when she was guiding her blind father; none knew better all his favorite walks in and around the beautiful country place where they lived; and her gentle, patient ways made her the very darling of his heart.

"In a few years there was another little being in the world, to whose happiness Ruth was necessary; and that was her poor blind cousin, Eva, and though Ruth's parents missed her sadly, they would often give up their darling, and send or take her into the city, to visit and comfort and amuse Eva.

"Ruth understood Eva better than any one else, because she had been her dear blind father's constant companion; and Eva loved her with all her heart; she knew her step;

she would hear it before any one else did, and the color would rush in her face, and she would wait with beating heart till the door opened, and then she would rush to her, throw her arms round her neck, and cry, 'Oh, dear Ruth! darling Ruth!' and kiss her twenty times, and Ruth would kiss Eva just as many, and then they would sit down close together, and have such a nice, happy talk! for Ruth had to tell all about the chickens, and Dandy, the pony, who loved sugar so dearly; and how she had hemmed six pocket-handkerchiefs for her dear father, and most wore a hole in her little thimble; and how her little baby brother had scrabbled off with old Dobbin's bran-bag, just as the poor old horse was

going to eat his dinner, and poked his own
dear little head in it, and when he pulled it
out, the bran was all over his face, making
him look as if he was covered with freckles;
which funny caper made Eva laugh like 'any
thing.'

"And when the talking was over, Ruth
read to little Eva, for all toys were useless to
the blind child; but her books were doubly
dear, and Ruth was never tired of reading
to her; so while she staid, Eva was as happy
as it was possible to be.

"One day the good doctor brought a
celebrated occulist to see Eva. An occulist
is a physician who cures diseases of the
eyes, and devotes his whole time and talent
to that precious and delicate part of the human frame.

"The occulist examined her eyes very carefully, and then said: 'After a few years I can perform an operation on Eva's eyes that *may* give her sight; but it will be a very painful one, and perhaps I may not succeed. If this dear little child were mine, I would almost rather let her remain blind than give her such terrible pain, which may end in disappointment.'

"But oh! what a blessed hope! her parents *would not* see the dark side; they dwelt upon the happiness it would be for little Eva to see; and one day her father took her upon his knee, and, fondly kissing her, said: 'Eva, my darling, would you like to see the beautiful sunlight and sweet flowers?'

"'O papa! yes! yes! but, most of all,

I want to see you and mamma, and Ruth and Dinah.'

" 'Well, my darling, if you can make up your mind to endure a terrible pain, when you are older we will have the operation tried. It will only last a moment, dear Eva, and then just think! you will see the whole beautiful world! and know all of us by our faces, as you now do by our steps and voices; you will see the birds flying in the air; the moon sailing slowly in the heavens, the little twinkling stars, and the rippling water, and we shall be so happy! so happy! I will not tell you when to have it done; I will wait till *you* are ready, my darling.'

"Then Eva thought long of it, and had many an earnest conversation upon the sub-

EVA PRAYING FOR STRENGTH TO SAY THE WORDS.

ject with her little cousin Ruth; and one day she said: 'Ruth, will you promise me, *true for true*, that you will come and hold my hand when they operate upon my eyes?'

" 'I promise you, *true for true*,' said Ruth.

" And so the matter was settled.

" Time passed on; and Eva was now eleven years old, and Ruth nine.

" Then Eva made a great resolution, and going to her father, she said: ' *Father, I am ready* now.'

" They were simple words; but poor little Eva had prayed to God, for nights and nights, and many times in the day, to give her strength to say them, and God had heard her prayer; for though her father turned

7

deadly pale at the words, the low sweet voice of the child did not tremble.

"And now the good doctor came, all his roughness gone, and he held that little head, with its glossy waves of hair, to keep it steady, but it trembled far less than he did; for he had watched Eva from her infancy, and dearly loved her, and he was intensely interested in the result of the experiment about to be performed.

"Near Eva stood her mother and her brave and faithful cousin Ruth, holding her hand, as she had promised '*true for true*,' and telling her to take courage, for all would be well.

"'Patience,' said the operator, softly; 'a pang, and half the suffering will be over.'

"The little hand which held Ruth's was clasped more tightly, and a groan smote on the listeners' ears. The room reeled—a faintness came over the heroic child; but she was soon herself again.

"'Would you not rather wait a day or two for the other eye to be operated upon?' said the kind physician. 'A week hence, or a month, will answer.'

"'Oh! no,' answered Eva, with quiet self-possession, 'let it be done to-day; let it be done NOW. I do not think I could bear the suspense, and it would *please my father* to know that it was over.'

"Love sustained her. Another sigh—another groan, and it was finished.

"Then came the bandages, the darkened

room, the stillness, the repose, for one whose nerves had been so shaken; but often those little cousinly hands were clasped together in a pressure which spoke more love than many words.

"Her father hardly ever left the house, and her mother wept often, for she loved her child in her blindness as much as a mother *could* love, and had never wished her to go through so much suffering—suffering which might be fruitless; and she waited for the result with trembling anxiety.

"A *look* from a physician has often more weight than many words spoken; and Ruth, who read the good doctor's face with the keenness of a child's perception, was the first to see an expression of hope shining upon it. When the day came for the bandages to be removed, Eva's father and mother were so dreadfully agitated, that they had to leave the room. Trembling, they stood out-side in the hall, waiting for the happy or wretched tidings.

"But Ruth—brave little Ruth—held Eva's hand as before. Those little clasped hands gave each other courage, for Ruth needed it as much as Eva, and her heart-beats could almost be heard in the silence. What a study her sweet little face was, as the emotions of love, pity, fear, and hope, crossed it, as shadowy clouds flit across the sky!

"Slowly, cautiously, the bandages were removed, and at last the end came, and the little girl saw upon the physician's face a broad, cheerful, happy smile. Ruth was a heroine, and had great self-control; but now control became impossible. She thought not of consequences—she only thought of the unceasing prayer which had been breathed by that household for many weeks—she only saw that that prayer had been granted.

"'SHE WILL SEE! she will see!!' she almost screamed. 'Eva! Eva! love! darling! do you hear?'

"The physician gave her a stern look of rebuke, but it was too late; Little Eva had fainted.

"'*Ruth is right*,' said he to the father and mother, who had rushed in at this blessed announcement, 'but she has been too abrupt. Her cousin and herself are wonderful little women in times of trial and danger; but neither of them are equal to a sudden joy.'

"It was a long time before Eva got well, and was permitted to use her new and precious gift o. sight; but then the amazement and delight with which she ran from one thing to another—the joy with which she gazed upon the faces of her parents and Ruth, no one of us, who have always seen, can ever know or appreciate.

"And old Binah said, as she hugged her darling to her faithful breast, 'God bress de good massa dat gib de sight to my little missis. It don't make no sort of difference to she, case old Binah *black*. Dear, no! she

lub her just de same when she see *dat!* don't
you, little missis?'

"'Why, *of course* I do,' answered little
Eva, and she kissed good old Binah, and ran
off with Ruth to look at some flowers. Oh,
that precious sight! how dear it was to
her!'

"And now she is no longer *poor* rich little Eva."

The children had listened to the story
of Eva, with eager, breathless attention; and
when Ruth screamed out, "She will see! she
will see!" they very nearly screamed, too,
so rejoiced were they that the blindness had
been removed; and the dear little girl had
not suffered so much for nothing.

"It must be so terrible to be blind," said Anna; " don't you remember when we went to see the exhibition of the blind children at the Academy of Music, the tears were rolling down mamma's face nearly the whole time, and we all felt so sorry, that we came home quite unhappy ?"

"Dear me," cried Harry, "I do wish there was no such affliction; why must there be, mamma ! "

"God knows best, dear Harry," answered the little mother. " If He did not, for His own wise purpose, permit us to know trouble and sorrow in this world, we would never desire that blessed rest and peace hereafter, which he promises to all those who put their trust in him."

"Yes, God must know best," said Clara, in a low voice; "for dear Charley has had more suffering and sorrow than any of us, and yet he loves Him, and wants to go to heaven."

"When Charley was very little," said the mother, "I found him crying bitterly one day. 'Why, what is the matter, my darling?' I said.

"'Oh mamma!' he sobbed, 'I am so afraid there won't be room enough in heaven for me! Do you think such a poor, lame child can get there?'

"I took him in my arms, and kissed and comforted him, and told him that Jesus looked at the heart, not at the weak, crooked body; and that the better and purer his life

was, the greater would be his welcome to
His house Beautiful, when life . had ended
here."

All the children looked at Charley, with
their eyes full of love; and in their prayers
that night, they entreated that Jesus would
remember their dear little brother's life-long
suffering, and give him a place close to Him
in heaven.

THE FOURTH LETTER.

ILL TEMPER.

For George.

"DEAR GEORGE:—You know you are now nearly seventeen years old, and quite a patriarch in the Nightcap family; and I am rejoiced that I can say with truth, that you have been, and are, a most excellent elder brother, unselfish, sweet-tempered, and always setting a good example."

"Dear me," interrupted George, laughing

and blushing very much, "I do not deserve such high praise;" but here the expression of his face changed, his lip began to tremble, and running up to his mother, he kissed her, and said—"Whatever I am that is good, you, dear mother, have made me."

"With God's help and blessing, my dear son," said his mother, returning the kiss; and then she went on reading.

"When you were a little fellow, of not quite seven years, you had the scarlet fever, and were very ill; and perhaps you remember how cross you were for a long time after."

"Oh, yes," exclaimed George; "mother used to say somebody else must have jumped into my skin, for, certainly, I was not the same George."

"I have written a story about this change in temper, and how a cure was effected. *You* became sweet-tempered again, as soon as you got quite well; but Arthur, in my story, required a lesson and some punishment, as he became cross without scarlet fever, rhyme, or reason. I hope you will let me know if you think I have invented a good plan to cure a cross-patch. You know I am a great believer in our always trying first upon *ourselves*, what we propose to '*do to others*,' as the very best way of finding out if we would like the same '*done to us*.'"

"Why, that's the 'golden rule!'" cried little Minnie; and now the children settled themselves, and eagerly listened to the following story:

ILL TEMPER.

" When Arthur was about seven years old, he was one of the very best boys to be found in a long summer's day. In the morning he would spring out of bed with a bright smile, wash and dress himself quickly, with the help of Mary, his kind nurse, say his prayers slowly and reverently, (ah! *that* was the secret of his goodness!) and then all day long he would be so obliging and good-tempered, that no one could help loving him that knew him; and so they didn't try to help it, for everybody loved him dearly.

" But, alas! I have heard the doctors say, (and of course *they* must know,) that once in every seven years the whole body is renewed, flesh, bones, blood, nerves, muscles; and I grieve to have to relate, that in Arthur's case the change seemed to include his spirit-part also; that is, his good temper and loving ways marched out of him, and some very bad substitutes marched in, as I shall proceed to relate.

"One morning Arthur awoke at his usual hour, but not with his usual smile. His face was all puckered up like a frozen apple. He floundered about the bed, and bumped his head against the head-board, and was just as cross as forty bears.

"Of course every thing went wrong; he put his stockings on wrongside out, tied his shoes in a hard knot, pulled on his pantaloons with the back part before, and drew his arms through his jacket upside down. Did you ever hear of such a piece of work?

"When Mary came to brush his hair and wash his face, he screamed out, stamping his foot at her—'Do stop! Stop! I tell you! You brush me as hard as ever you can! I wish you would leave me alone, you ugly old thing!'

"Oh, dear, dear, what a sad boy! He puts me in mind of that other naughty boy who scolded his nurse in a piece of poetry. This is it:

"'Oh *why* must my face be washed so clean,
  And scrubbed and scoured for Sunday?
When you know very well, as you've always seen,
  'Twill be dirty again on Monday.

8

" ' My hair is stiff with the hateful soap,
That behind my ears is dripping;
My smarting eyes, I'm afraid to ope,
And my lips the suds are sipping.

" ' They're down my throat, and they're up my nose,
And to choke me you seem to be trying,
That I'll shut my mouth, you needn't suppose,
For how can I keep from crying?

" ' And you rub as hard as ever you can,
And your hands are hard, to my sorrow;
No woman shall wash me, when I'm a man,
And I wish I was one to-morrow.'

"But at last Arthur went sulking down to breakfast, *forgetting to say his prayers;* and taking his seat at the table, whined out, the very first thing—'Just look at this piece of toast; it is all burnt, and as hard as a stone. I won't have it!' Then he tasted his coffee, and exclaimed—'Pooh! what coffee! perfect slops!'

"His mother was grieved to see him acting so naughtily, and said, gently—'I am sorry, Arthur, you are not pleased; will you have an egg?'

"Arthur cracked an egg with his teaspoon, looked at it, threw it down, and turning up his nose with disdain, said—'Eggs! Brickbats you mean! they have been boiling all night.'

"This exhibition of ill temper distressed his mother exceedingly, but she did not say any thing to him then; being a woman of excellent sense, she formed a plan in her mind which she hoped would effect a cure.

"Arthur was an only child. His parents were rich, and they preferred that he should be educated at home; they feared his learning evil as well as good at a large school. Hitherto this plan had been very successful, for Arthur was as studious and obedient as his tutors could possibly wish; and this sudden and sad change made all around him unhappy. I will give you a history of one of these miserable days.

"On this morning, his tutor arrived, as usual, at nine o'clock; and commenced by giving his pupil a lesson in penmanship. There was an ominous scowl on Arthur's face. He twitched his copy-book before him, pretended he could not find a good pen, scratched and blotted the paper from top to bottom, and so, when the lesson was finished, the page was a sight to behold.

" ' You have not tried to write well,' said his master, mildly.

" ' My pen was abominable, and the paper was greasy,' said Arthur, sulkily.

" ' A bad workman always pretends that his *tools* are to blame,' said the master.

" ' Oh, dear me! you are never satisfied! If I write too lightly, you say it looks as if a spider had scampered over the paper with inky legs; if I bear on harder, you ask me how much horse power I have put on to make such heavy strokes. I don't know what to do! I don't! You are always grumbling.'

" ' Oh, no! not always, for here are a great

many pages on which I have written, 'Very well; very well, indeed.'

" ' That was only by chance,' said Arthur.

" ' But if these chances do not always occur, whose fault is it ? '

" ' Oh, mine! I suppose you mean to say,' answered Arthur, pettishly.

" ' Well, my dear boy, only look at your writing to-day. It resembles a company of soldiers, each of whom carries his musket to suit himself, this one to the right, that to the left, a third horizontally, a fourth perpendicularly, and all the rest of the letters with broken backs and crooked legs. Just look at it ! '

" ' Oh, dear ! you are always mocking me,' whined Arthur. ' One would think I did it all on purpose. Oh, dear me!'

"At last this lesson came to an end; but the others were no better, and the poor master went away with his temper sorely tried, sadly remembering the happy and good little Arthur of the year before.

"In the afternoon, his mother said, in a pleasant tone, 'Come, dear Arthur, come and take a walk with me; it is such a lovely day; the robins are singing in the trees; and look, how fast the delicate white clouds are sailing through the air! Come, dear.'

"'It isn't pleasant! and I can't *bear* robins,' said Arthur.

"His mother sighed and went alone.

"Left at home, Arthur tried to amuse himself. He got out his puzzle, or dissected map of the United States; but as ill-tempered people are never patient or gentle, in a very little while he had cracked South Carolina nearly in two, snapped off the top of Maryland, broken New York into three pieces, and made mince-meat of the Union generally, which was a very shocking thing to do, even on a dissected map; and then, the cross boy ended by throwing all the States into the black coal-scuttle.

"After this he tried to read; but nothing seemed to amuse him. From 'Robinson Crusoe' he went to the 'Rollo Books,' and from those to 'Nightcaps,' and declared they were all stupid alike, 'a perfect pack of nonsense!'

"As a last resource, he called Jumbo, his big cat, who was so fond of Arthur, that he

would let him do just what he pleased with
him, that is, as long as his little master was
kind; but to-day he pinched his ears, and
pulled his tail, and twitched his whiskers at
such a rate, that poor Jumbo puckered up
his face like a pudding-bag, and squalled like
a first-class opera singer.

"'The bad old thing!' exclaimed Arthur.
'I declare, he ought to be drowned! I'll
never play with him again. Scat! scat! get
out!' and off scampered poor Jumbo, and hid
himself behind the kitchen door.

"All this time you are wondering his
mother did not punish him. Wait a little.
Just read to the end, and then tell me what
you think of her mode of punishment. I shall
wish very much to know if you approve of it.

" One evening, after Arthur had gone to bed, his father and mother had a long consultation with each other about the best way of curing Arthur's ill temper; and they agreed upon a plan his mother had thought of during the day.

" The next morning came, when the trial was to be made. Every one received his or her instructions from Arthur's mother, and were quite ready to begin the new mode of punishment.

" But, for a wonder, on this particular morning Arthur awoke feeling very pleasant and amiable. Never mind, he was to receive his lesson all the same.

" While Mary was helping him to dress, she seemed very snappish and impatient.

ARTHUR'S MOTHER TELLING HER PLAN.

" 'Do, for goodness sake, keep still, Master Arthur!' she said; 'you are always fidgeting and fussing.'

" '*I?*' said Arthur, laughing. 'Why, I've been as still as a mouse!'

" Mary was silent for a moment, but presently she exclaimed—'How carelessly you have washed your hands, your shirt is all wet. I have shown you how to wash without splashing a hundred times. You worry my life out!'

" 'I *tried* to do as you told me,' said Arthur, with a little sigh.

" 'Oh, fiddlesticks! don't tell *me!* You are a terrible boy!' and Mary bounced out of the room, banging the door behind her.

" Arthur went down to breakfast, and

ran up to his mother to tell her about Mary. 'I think *she* was "terrible,"' he said. 'What could be the matter with her, mamma?'

"'Perhaps she was indulging in ILL TEMPER,' answered his mother, significantly.

"When they sat down to breakfast there was no toast.

"'I should like a piece of toast,' said Arthur.

"His mother rang a little bell, and the cook came in. She looked first at the mistress, with a peculiar smile, and then she looked at Arthur.

"'Margaret,' said he, 'there is no toast.'

"'I know it, Master Arthur; it was too brown; and you are so hard to suit, that I did not dare to serve it.'

" '*I* hard to suit?' cried Arthur, who seemed to have forgotten what a naughty boy he had been. '*I* hard to suit? Not at all. If the toast *is* a little too brown, I don't mind it. Give it to me, Margaret.'

" 'I threw it away,' said the cook.

" 'Oh, well, I'm in no hurry; I will wait while you make me another piece.'

" 'My fire has gone out,' said the cook.

" 'Well, you can re-light it, can't you?'

" 'Do you think I have nothing to do but to wait upon you?' cried the cook. 'You know nothing ever suits you; and you always speak rudely to me;' and she flounced out of the room.

" 'How *can* she say so, mamma?' cried Arthur. '*I* speak rudely to her? Why, I was as polite as ever I could be. It is too bad!'

"'Servants find it very hard to attend upon you, Arthur. They are accustomed to polite treatment from the rest of us.'

"'Well—but mamma—to accuse me to-day, when it was *she* who '—

"'Was indulging in ILL-TEMPER,' interrupted his mother.

"*Arthur understood*, and was silent.

"The hour for his grammar lesson had now arrived. The tutor bowed to Arthur's mother, smiled, and commenced:

"'Do you know your lessons, my young friend?'

"'I have studied them, sir.'

"'Do you *know* them? It is of little

consequence that you have studied them, if you do not know them.'

" 'I believe I do, sir.'

" ' Well, let us see—begin.'

" 'In the *tenses*,' began Arthur a little embarrassed, 'we should distinguish the *moods* and the verbs.'

" 'Nonsense ! you should have said, " In the *verbs* we should distinguish the moods and the tenses." '

" ' Yes, sir, that is what I *meant* to say ; I knew that, but my tongue slipped.'

" 'Your tongue slips very often. Continue'—

" Arthur, still more embarrased, said— 'We should also distinguish the *moods* and the persons.'

" 'You must be demented! What have the moods to do in that sentence? Perhaps you are expecting a visit from the man in the moon, and that makes you talk such nonsense. The grammar says—"We should distinguish the *numbers* and the persons." Your tongue does nothing but slip; you do not know your lesson.'

" ' Excuse me, sir; I do know it.'

" ' You are not respectful, Master Arthur,' said the teacher in a cold, severe tone.

" ' But, sir'—

" ' When a boy knows his lesson he does not make such abominable blunders in reciting.'

" ' But, sir, you troubled me; you put me out.'

"'*I* trouble you? A very singular excuse, and a very poor one. Come, let me look at your composition.'

"But here matters became worse and worse. The master 'pshawed,' and frowned, and grumbled to himself. 'No application! no thought! bad spelling! bad grammar! a perfect mass of faults!'

"Arthur grew red and pale by turns, as his teacher wrote right across the page in large letters: 'A composition so badly done, that it is impossible to correct it.'

"Then he rose coldly, looking very grim, took his hat, and addressing Arthur's mother, said—'Madam, I cannot consent to teach your son any longer; I have so little success, that I feel I have no right to the very

9

liberal salary you have accorded me. Another, perhaps, will do better.'

" 'Oh, sir! no! pray, don't go!' exclaimed Arthur; 'I will try to do better! indeed, I will! upon my word and honor I will. I love you, sir!'

" A pleasant light suddenly came into the teacher's eyes, and a soft smile passed like lightning over his lips.

" 'Do, please, give me your hand, sir,' said Arthur, 'and promise me that you will continue to teach me.'

" His broad, black eyebrows immediately contracted into a great frown; and he said gruffly—'Very well, I will try you once more,' and left the room.

" For a few moments there was silence;

then a distressed expression came over Arthur's face, as he said—'Mamma, my teacher was very— (he was at a loss for a word) very *singular* with me to-day—don't you think so, mamma?'

" ' What do you mean by *singular?*

" ' Why, not as he usually is—not at all.'

" ' His reproofs seemed perfectly just to me; you were not perfect in your lessons.'

" ' Well, mamma, I do not deny that; but at all other times he has been so kind and patient, and never treated me with such unexpected severity.'

" ' Ah!' said his mother, 'I am afraid, then, that this morning he was indulging in ILL TEMPER.'

"Arthur hung his head, and was silent: his conscience was busy whispering to him, and the rest of the morning passed painfully; but after luncheon, he prepared for a walk with joy, for the day was lovely, and the air exhilarating.

" But all at once the sky became overcast, and very soon after the rain fell in torrents.

" ' Oh, dear me, how tiresome! ' cried Arthur, 'just when I am going to take a walk; it is perfectly hateful.'

" ' God sends the rain,' said his mother, gently.

" Arthur hung his head again without answering. What could he say, indeed? But with his new resolution strong in his mind, he determined to bear this disappointment with patience; and he called Jumbo to play with him.

"But the cat, usually so quick to come purring to his knee, remained just where he was, as if he had been suddenly struck deaf, and dumb, and blind. Arthur went to him, and tried to take him in his arms; but he hissed at his playmate, and scampered away with his back and tail high in the air, and hid under the sofa.

"'Ah me!' sighed Arthur, 'I suppose Jumbo is like the rest; he is indulging in ILL TEMPER, too.'

"'Not quite that,' observed his mother; 'but animals have *memories*.'

"'I think you had better say that they are spiteful, mamma.'

"'Perhaps they are, my son; but they have no reason, while *we* are capable of controlling our impatience, and governing our passions, if we ask God to help us.'

"Upon this Arthur fairly broke down; and, bursting into tears, sobbed out—'Oh, dear mamma, I understand the lesson I have received from every one to-day. Do believe that I will try with all my strength to conquer my ill temper: I promise you. Do, please mamma, forgive me.'

"His mother wound her loving arms around her son, and tenderly kissed him, and said—'I forgive you, my dear child, with all my heart, and we will both pray to our Heavenly Father to send down His Holy Spirit to guide and direct your efforts to do right.

You have borne your disappointments to-day with patience and resignation; and I feel that you will soon be the good, sweet-tempered boy, you were a year ago.'

" Arthur kept his promise, and whenever he was tempted to give a cross answer, or get in a passion, he was sure to remember in time the celebrated day when everybody, by his mother's instructions, attempted his cure, by showing him, in their own persons, the unlovely consequences of indulging in

ILL TEMPER."

" What a nice story!" exclaimed the children, " and what a good way of curing Arthur—better than a hundred whippings.

When we do any thing bad, mamma, you must punish us Aunt Fanny's way. Couldn't you punish us for something now?"

The little mother laughed at this comical request, and said—"I can't think of any thing just now to punish you for; and I hope you don't want to do any thing naughty on purpose."

"O dear, no!" cried the children, but George, with a good-humored twinkle in his eye, added—"At any rate, mamma, the next time Harry puts salt into the sugar-bowl, and makes me spoil my coffee, I intend to put powdered sugar into the salt-cellar for him to sprinkle over his stewed oysters."

"Oh, do!" cried all the children; "only think of oysters and sugar! perfectly dreadful!"

" 'Well,' said Harry, laughing, 'I shall have to buy a snuff-box, then, and keep it in my pocket full of salt.'

" 'But don't forget yourself,' said Anna, 'and politely offer a pinch of it to the first old lady you meet; she might think you meant to play a trick upon her, you know.'

" 'What an idea!' cried Harry; 'I wouldn't do such a thing; I should think it would make her sneeze worse than any snuff. Wouldn't it?'

" 'The best way to find that out,' said George, with a roguish smile, 'would be to take a good pinch yourself.'

" While this conversation had been going on, little Johnny had disappeared in the pantry; and now, at this very moment, he came out, screaming: 'Oh! my nose hurts! my nose hurts!' and ran to his mother.

"It seems that, anxious to find out what kind of snuff salt would make, he had privately walked into the pantry, and had snuffed and poked quite a quantity into his poor little nose, and now it smarted as if twenty hornets had stung him at once; and he jumped up and down with the pain.

"They had a great time soaking his nose in warm water, and felt very sorry for him, though they could not, for their lives, help laughing when George said that Johnny had salted and pickled his nose so well, that it would keep in the hottest weather; at any rate, it would last him as long as he lived; which comforted Johnny very much, for he thought that it might have to be cut off to get the salt out.

"After this they bid everybody good night, and went to bed, and Johnny said he felt 'pretty *compertuffle.*' His mother had told him that 'good little Henry,' of whom you have read, always said 'compertuffle' for 'comfortable,' and Johnny thought it was just the right word to express his feelings."

THE FIFTH LETTER.

THE ROSE CROWN.

For Clara.

Dear, tender-hearted little Clara:—
In the olden time, there was a beautiful
superstition in Germany, that on Christmas
eve our Saviour, just as he was when a little
child here below, comes at midnight in at
the door, and fills all those children's shoes
with gifts, who have followed His example
of goodness and obedience.   You know that

Note.—This story was suggested by reading about Christmas in Germany, in Bayard Taylor's "Views Afoot."

you hang up your *stockings*, and Santa Claus comes down the chimney; but the little German children believe that they are far more blessed. It is a beautiful idea, for it brings Him, who for our sakes became a little child on earth, more closely and lovingly to the children's hearts. They grow up sure of His love and sympathy, from infancy to old age.

I have asked Sarah ("the doctor") to write me another story after the German fashion, on purpose for you. She has given me this "Rose Crown;" and the story turns upon the sweet and solemn belief of the German children.

You will perceive that the little Gottfried in the story thought of this with such intensity, and with such perfect faith in its truth, as to cause him to walk in his sleep, like a somnambulist. No doubt your dear mother can tell you many strange and extraordinary stories of somnambulists, who do the most wonderful and startling things while in this kind of trance state, of which they are utterly unconscious when they awake.

I hope this story will please my dear little Clara; it is called

THE ROSE CROWN.

" It was Christmas eve, and a cold winter's day. The flakes of snow fell softly and thickly, and had already covered the earth with a white cloak.

" At one of the windows of the large house that stands on the top of the hill, where the purple violets first peep out in the spring-time, stood the little Gottfried and his sister Marie.

" ' Only look, dear Marie,' said Gottfried, 'how fast the snow falls! What large flakes! They look like little milk-white doves.'

" ' It is the Mother Holle shaking her feather-beds,' cried Marie, laughing; and looking up towards the sky, and beckoning with her hand, she sang—

> " ' Mother Holle,
>   Good wife Holle,
> Fill the meadows fair and full:
>   Stay not, pause not,
>   Shake away,
> Make the snow fall fast to-day.'

"'Oh! I can sing a prettier song than thine,' said Gottfried. 'Listen, now. The good wife Katarine taught it to me; and he sang—

"'See the snow-flakes,
    Merry snow-flakes!
How they fall from yonder sky,
Coming lightly, coming sprightly,
Dancing downwards, from on high.
Faint or tire, will they never,
Wheeling round and round forever.
    Surely nothing do I know,
    Half so merry as the snow;
Half so merry, merry, merry,
    As the dancing, glancing snow.

"'See the snow-flakes,
    Solemn snow-flakes!
How they whiten, melt and die.

In what cold and shroud-like masses
O'er the buried earth they lie.
Lie as though the frozen plain
Ne'er would bloom with flowers again.
  Surely nothing do I know,
  Half so solemn as the snow,
Half so solemn, solemn, solemn,
    As the falling, melting snow.'

"'Ah! thy song is sad, brother,' said little Marie: 'it makes me sigh.'

"As she spoke, a little boy, poorly clad, was seen coming up the avenue; and Gottfried exclaimed—'Here comes Heinrich!' and running out of the room, he presently returned, leading by the hand Heinrich, the little faggot-maker, whose mother, a poor but pious widow, lived in a hut just out of the village.

10

" ' Why, Heinrich, where hast thou been this cold day ? ' asked Marie.

" ' Taking my faggots to Herr Kaufferman's,' said the poor boy. ' But oh, Gottfried, they have there the most beautiful Christmas Tree ! ' and then Heinrich paused and sighed.

" ' And to-night the dear Christ-kind-cherr, or Holy Child, will bring them presents,' said Gottfried. ' I hope he will fill *thy* shoes full.' *

" ' Alas ! the Christ-child never comes to me,' said Heinrich.

" ' What ! hast thou never heard how he comes at midnight, bearing a lighted taper

---

* In Germany, they fill the children's shoes instead of their stockings.

THE BAD BOY TAUNTING HEINRICH.

and a crown of white roses, and gives presents to all the good children?'

" 'My mother has told me of this,' said Heinrich, ' and I have waited and watched, but he *never* comes! He never *will* come. It was only yesterday that I met Hans, the butcher's son, and he mocked me, and snapped his fingers in my face, and said—"Thou art so poor, that thy shoes will never have any thing in them;" and I was so angry, and wanted to strike him, but my mother said I must never fight or quarrel with any one, and I went away from him; but it is hard to be poor,' and here he began to cry.

" ' Ah! yes, it is sad, dear Heinrich; but do not weep; here, wipe thine eyes with my new pocket-handkerchief. Come, now, be happy; and I will pray to the Christ-child, and beg him to come this very night to thee.'

" At this the little faggot-maker's face brightened, and soon after he went away.

" In the evening, the children had their supper, and soon after they stood by the knee of their kind mother, and sang this hymn:

" Jesus, our Shepherd ! we ask for thy blessing,
    Through the long hours of this dreary night;
Let us not know (thy kind favor possessing)
    Danger or sorrow, till morning is bright.

" Jesus, our Saviour ! oh ! grant thy protection,
    To thy dear arms we have trustingly come;
Oh, Lamb of God ! make secure our election,
    Guard us, and keep us, and call us thine own.

" Jesus, our Crown ! Oh, thou Heavenly Glory !
    Humbly we kneel, and entreat thee to love,
Bless and receive us, as in Bible story,
    Till we shall come to thy mansion above."

" When they had finished the hymn, they reverently repeated their prayers ; and then, each bidding the other good night and sweet dreams, went to their white-curtained beds.

" Later at night, their mother came to see that they were warm. Gottfried was still awake ; he was troubled about little Heinrich ; and he told his mother how the poor boy had grieved because the Christ-child never came to him. 'I have prayed to Him, dear mother ; do you think He will hear me ?' said the tender-hearted boy.

" ' Yes, dear child,' said the mother, ' dost thou not remember what the hymn says?

> " And when, dear Jesus, I kneel down,
>   Morning and night to prayer,
>   Something there is within my heart,
>   Which tells me THOU ART THERE."

" ' He works sometimes through *human* hands; and now look thou, my little Gottfried,' continued his mother, kissing him, ' I will make this night a wreath of white roses for thee, and fasten a purse about the stems, with some golden guilders within, and thou shalt take it to Heinrich to-morrow morning.'

" ' Ah, thou dearest mother!' cried Gottfried, joyfully, and the loving kisses were

pressed upon her cheek. 'The dear Jesus
has heard me already;' and kneeling in the
bed, he poured out his grateful thanks; and
then lying down, he soon fell asleep, with a
bright flush of happiness upon his face.

"The snow had ceased to fall, and it was
late, but still in the widow's cottage the fit-
ful fire-light (for candles there were none)
showed her bending over some work. By
her side on the hearth crouched the little
Heinrich.

"'Go to bed, dear child,' said his mother;
'it is too late for thee.'

"'Ah, dear mother! let me wait for
thee,' answered the boy; 'it is so cold and
dark in our little room above.' He was silent

for a moment, gazing into the fire in a wishful manner; then he said—'Mother, dost thou think the Christ-child will indeed hear Gottfried's prayer, and come to me and thee?'

"'I hope he will, my Heinrich,' said the sad mother, smiling faintly.

"'Ah, but mother, dost thou not *know* it?'

"The fire burned low, and the poor woman could no longer see. She put up the coarse sewing with a sigh, and resting her hand tenderly on her boy's head, sat quite still.

"Not a sound was heard. The light in the room was dim, and gloom had settled upon the hearts of both mother and child.

"Hark! what was that?

"A low tap sounded at the door, and then it slowly opened; and to the astonished gaze of the two sitting by the hearth, there appeared the figure of a little child. A snow-white robe draped his slender limbs. In one hand he bore a lighted taper, and in the other a most beautiful wreath of white roses. His dark blue eyes shone with an unearthly lustre, as it appeared to the amazed and bewildered Heinrich, and his golden curls floated upon his shoulders.

"'Oh! mother! mother!' whispered Heinrich, almost breathless, 'it is the Christ-child in very truth come to me at last. His face is like Gottfried's—only far more beautiful;' and mother and son sank on their knees.

"Slowly the little form advanced towards them, paused before Heinrich, lightly placed the rose crown upon his head, and then, the sweet lips parting in a faint, tender smile, it waved its little hand towards him, and disappeared from their sight.

"When they could speak, the mother and son bowed their heads in thankful prayer, then lifted their brimming eyes to each other.

"'Truly thou hast been wondrously rewarded, my Heinrich,' said the poor widow; 'give the beautiful crown to me, that I may see what the dear Christ-child has brought to thee.'

"She stirred the fire, and put on some light wood to make a blaze, and then Heinrich lifted the crown from his head. As he

did so—oh! wonder! there fell from it a
silken purse, and through the deep crimson
network they could see the yellow gleam of
gold.

"With the early blush of morning little
Gottfried awoke, and the first thing he did
was to run smilingly to the door to find his
shoes. There they were, in good truth,
crammed to the very top with presents.
Marie, too, awoke at the moment, and from
each little white bed there arose delighted
exclamations and merry shouts of joy.

"Now their mother entered, and said—
'A merry Christmas to you, my children.'

"With joyful kisses they welcomed her,
and breathlessly showed her their gifts;

then Gottfried exclaimed—'Oh! mother! I have had such a pleasant dream; I dreamed that the dear Christ-child went to Heinrich with the wreath, and gave it to him.'

"'Well, thou shalt take it thyself this morning, dear child, when thou hast eaten thy breakfast.'

"But what was this? Where could the wreath be? The good mother, faithful to her promise had made it the evening before, and had laid it on the table in the parlor, but it was not to be found.

"This loss put the little Gottfried in such distress, that his mother promised quickly to make another; and she was just preparing to hasten out to purchase the roses, when Heinrich ran in, his mother following;

and, scarcely pausing for breath, the boy told the wonderful thing that had happened to them in the night.

"With a sudden understanding of the strange and beautiful story, Gottfried's mother took Heinrich's mother aside, and whispered to her how the rose crown had mysteriously disappeared from the house in the night.

"The two mothers gazed into each other's faces, and then looked with love and wonder at the little unconscious Gottfried. Tender tears and smiles struggled in their faces, for they knew in a moment that it was he who had risen in his sleep, had taken the rose crown to Heinrich, and had laid his head upon his pillow again without waking.

"When they gently and tenderly told the strange tale to the wondering children, Heinrich, bursting into tears, threw his arms passionately round Gottfried's neck, and sobbed out—' Oh! Gottfried! how thou must have loved me to have done this thing, even while sleeping;' and the grateful boy never forgot it. He kept his crown of roses as his dearest treasure, though they soon became withered and brown; and Gottfried and Heinrich were always friends, though one was rich and the other poor; and each mother loved and blessed the child of the other even as her own."

"A—h!" sighed the children, when the

story was finished; "this is the best of all! How those two German boys must have loved each other ever after."

"Gottfried must have been almost as good as Charley,"said Clara, with a glance full of love towards her brother. The little girl, with her sweet, sensitive nature, and gentle, caressing ways, seemed closer to Charley than the rest, though he loved all his brothers and sisters with his whole heart; but Clara was softer and tenderer, and murmured out her love in such a dove-like way, that, next to his mother, the sick boy liked to have her smooth his hair, and hold his hand, and kneel by his side in prayer; and the rest of the children knew this, and lovingly gave

Clara "her place." Not a shade of envy, that black and wicked passion, ever entered their hearts; for, as I have many times written, this was the home of LOVE.

THE SIXTH LETTER.

THE HUNT FOR A STEAMBOAT.

To Johnny.

DEAR LITTLE JOHNNY*:—I have heard such a cunning little story about two little children that live in New York, that I have written it out for you; I shall begin it, "Once upon a time"—the way you like best. Here it is:

THE HUNT FOR A STEAMBOAT.

"Once upon a time little Harry was playing in the parlor, and his kind mother was

11

reading. Presently the door opened, and a
lady entered, holding by the hand the dearest little bit of a girl you ever saw, about
three years old, with such sweet blue eyes
and soft curling hair, that she looked almost
like a fairy.

"Harry's mother was very glad to see
the lady; she kissed her and little Nannie,
and made them sit on the very best sofa, and
Harry kissed Nannie, and everybody seemed
very much pleased.

"After saying what a very fine day it was,
just as all the grown people do when they
begin to talk, Nannie's mamma began to tell
Harry's mamma something very wonderful,
when, all at once, they saw Harry's eyes
opened about as big round as a pair of

saucers, and a dozen ears seemed to have sprouted out all over his head; and he was listening to the wonderful story with every one of them.

"Harry's mamma thought that would never do, and she said—'My son, Nannie's mamma and I want to talk secrets, and it is not right for such a little boy as you to hear them; so take the dear little girl out of the room, and show her every thing she wants to see. Mind. dear! *show her every thing.*'

"So Harry took Nannie's hand, and led her out of the room. He felt quite bashful at first, and when he got into the hall and had shut the door, he dropped her hand; and then the two children stood and looked

at each other like two pussy cats on a fence;
only they looked a great deal prettier, because, you know, neither of them had any
fierce whiskers or long claws. Not they, indeed! I suppose Harry will have whiskers
one of these days, if he lives to be a man;
but Nannie will never have any, because if
she lives a thousand years she will never be
a great, rough man, but a beautiful little
woman, which is a great comfort to think of.

"At last Harry said—'Say, Nannie,
what do you want to see?'

"'I want to tee a 'teamboat.'

"'A steamboat!' exclaimed Harry.

"'Ess, a 'teamboat—big one!' said little
Nannie.

"Harry looked puzzled; but he took her

hand again, and led her very carefully up
the long flight of stairs, and into every room
on the second floor. They looked under the
beds and into the band-boxes, opened all the
bureau drawers and wardrobe doors, peer-
ed down into the bath-tub, and almost tumbled in, and couldn't find a steamboat. Then
they went up stairs again, and all over
the rooms in the third story—no steamboat
there.

"Then they went up stairs again, and all
over the rooms in the top of the house,
opened all the cook's bundles, the waiter's
boxes, the chambermaid's trunk, and the
laundress's umbrella; but not a single steamboat was to be seen.

"What was poor Harry to do?

"He *must* mind his mamma; and Nannie kept saying—'I want to tee a 'teamboat.'

" All of a sudden Harry spied a globe of the world in one corner of the attic, and he cried out—' Here, Nannie, let's look on this world and see if we can find one.'

"So down they nestled close together, and turned the world round and round, but, strange to tell, there was not a single steamboat sailing on it.   It was really too bad.

"They came down stairs again, and then a bright thought struck Harry—'Oh, yes!' he exclaimed, 'I know where a steamboat is. Dear me! certainly! Come, Nannie, hurry.'

"Down they went to the hall, and Harry put on his cap, and opened the front door, and the children went out. Hand in hand they trotted merrily along, both delighted to think that at last they were on the track of a steamboat.

"After walking a long way, they came to a rough board fence, and Harry peeped through a knot-hole to see what was inside. He looked so long, that Nannie cried impatiently—'Let me see the 'teamboat.'

"'No, it isn't,' said Harry; 'it's some boys playing ball. Come and look.'

"Nannie went close to the fence, and stood on the very tips of her little toes, but the knot-hole was too high; so Harry lifted her with all his strength, and she had a fine time seeing the boys playing ball.

"As he let her come down rather suddenly, she caught her frock in a splinter of wood in the fence, and it was torn from top to bottom. 'Oh, my!' said Nannie, looking at her dress, 'what a *gate* hole; oh, my!'

"Oh, never mind it,' cried Harry, 'that's nothing;' and he laughed so merrily, that Nannie thought to tear dresses was great fun, and laughed too.

"On they went, hand in hand, and every fence they came to where there were no houses, they peeped through and searched for the steamboat; and they scrambled and fell against so many rough boards, that Nannie's **pretty** little **new** hat that her kind grandmamma had just given her, was all bent and torn and twisted, till from a nice little round hat, it came to be a queer-looking, five-cornered one, with one end of ribbon over her nose, and another sticking out behind; and **the** beautiful lace cap inside was only fit for the rag-bag. Did you ever hear any thing like it?

"Well, the dear little things wandered on, Harry knowing that he was minding his mamma, like a good boy. He was very happy; because, you know, children that are obedient and good are never any thing else. Of course not.

"And little Nannie's lovely blue eyes were very busy looking all over the world for the steamboat.

"At last they came to an open space—I believe, in Seventy-second street, where the Central Park is; and a very amiable-looking policeman, who fortunately at that time was wide awake, happened to look that way.

"He was very much astonished when he saw such little creatures all alone; and Nannie, looking as if she had been in the wars; but, in spite of her torn dress, looking like just what she was—the tender little pet of a household, watched over, and loved, and cared for night and day; and Harry, too, it was plain to see, with his bright eyes and

manly bearing, was of gentle birth and breed-
ing.

"So the policeman walked up to them,
and said—'I suppose this is Tom Thumb and
his wife out for a walk.'

"'No, it isn't,' said Harry; ·my name is
Harry.'

"'And what is yours, little lady?'

"'My name 'ittle Nannie.'

"'Where did you come from?'

"'Home,' said Harry.

"'Where is home?'

"'Why, in Thirty-second street, to be
sure; don't you know?'

"'Did you run away?' said the policeman.

"'No,' said Harry, and his eyes blazed

with indignation, 'I'm minding mamma; she told me to show Nannie every thing, and Nannie wanted to see a steamboat, and I'm finding one for her now!'

"At this the policeman laughed, and then he looked so kindly at the children, that I suspect he had a dozen children of his own at his house, and that made him love every other little child. Why, bless your dear little heart, I love all the little children in the whole world, because I love you so dearly.

"Then the policeman said—'Well, Harry, you are a long way from home; and I think you had better put off the steamboat-hunting business till some other day. Your mother may think you and Nannie are a little too young to travel about the world by

THE STEAMBOAT HARRY AND EMMA WERE LOOKING FOR.

yourselves. Come; I will go back with you.

"It was very fortunate he did, for though Harry knew very well what street he lived in, he did not know how to get to it; and it would have been a sad thing for the dear little creatures if they had been lost. But now the good policeman took Nannie in his arms, because she was getting very tired, and Harry by the hand, and they all got into a railroad car, and before long were at the house.

"But oh! what a distracted house! For when Nannie's mother had finished the wonderful secret, and wanted to leave, the children were not to be found. They searched the house; they examined the bath-tubs and

wash-tubs; they went out into the garden
and down into the cellar, but they were not
to be found; and then the weeping, terrified
mothers went out into the street, and asked
everybody they met, if they had seen the
children.

"The waiter, who was just setting the
table for dinner, rushed round the corner,
brandishing the carving-knife like a pistol,

and frightened a fashionable young gentleman out of all his five wits, for he thought it

was a crazy man, trying to kill him; and
when he turned round he was scared again,
for there was the laundress, who had started
out with a wet shirt in her hands, which she
was just starching; there *she* was, waving it
about in the wind, like a flag of distress, and
crying as hard as she could.

"Then the waiter dropped the carving-
knife, and flew up the street, while the fat
cook, who had left a pudding half-made in
the kitchen, ran after him, dropping her pud-

ding-stick, and wheezing dreadfully; and away in the distance, they saw the chamber-maid, with the broomstick in her hand, and her hair all about her ears. - She looked so like a witch, from grief and fright, that as she disappeared, the people looking after her were sure she had mounted the broomstick the very next moment, and had flown over the tops of the houses.

"Dear me! what a terrible time it was! But you see they all loved Harry so much, that they were almost crazy, and that made them cut up all these didoes.

"All came back lamenting, for no children had been found; and the distressed mothers were just writing a note to send to the police-office, to order the whole city to be searched,

when—a quick ring at the bell— Could it
be? Out they all rushed, mothers, cook,
waiter, chambermaid, laundress, the cat, and
the dog. The door was opened, and, oh, joyful sight! there stood the children and the
policeman, all laughing together.

" No wonder they all screamed and cried,
and laughed and talked, all in a bunch. Nobody cared a pin for Nannie's torn dress and
five-cornered bonnet, when the darling child
was safe, and hugged tight to her mother's
breast; and Harry and his mother had a
grand kissing time too. Why, dear me!
they almost wanted to kiss the good policeman, they were so glad; not quite, though;
but they gave him what he thought was
quite astonishing—something that came out

12

of a purse, and shone like gold; and between you and me, it *was* gold.

"And Harry's mother was not the least angry with him, when she heard that he was such a good boy, and was only minding his mamma when he went all over the world with Nannie to find a steamboat: no, indeed! She kissed him again. But let me tell you as a great secret, that she was very careful after that to tell Harry to look for steamboats, or any thing else little girls or he might want to see, *inside* of the house; and although it is many months since this happened, I know that Harry and Nannie have not been steamboat-hunting since; but they are both good, lovely children, and both mind their mammas."

"Oh, dear!" exclaimed Johnny, "*my* story is tip-top! I wish you would read it right over again, mamma."

"Yes, mamma, do!" cried all the rest. "It is *so* interesting. Dear little Nannie, she's a darling!"

"I wonder if her grandmother gave her a new hat," said Minnie. "*I* would, if *I* was her grandmother."

The children laughed at the idea of Minnie's being a grandmother, and Harry said —"Come, sit on my lap, grandmother, and let me see if you know your letters yet." Minnie did not like this much, but as Harry called her his "dear little pet" the next moment, she forgave him immediately.

"But Aunt Fanny has written something

else in this letter," said the mother. "Shall I read it, or repeat the story?"

"Oh! read all the letter *this time*," cried the children, " and the story again to-morrow night."

The little mother read on.

" And now, my dear children, I have sent you six stories; and if any one will count the boots and shoes in the first Nightcap book, they will 'find that there are the surprising number of thirteen of you!—a baker's dozen.

" Let me see how many are left.

" Minnie and Willie, and Bennie and Lillie, and dear little Fanny, my *namesake, and Katie and Pet*. I think I will write to this dear little band collectively, and the

stories shall make the 'Little Nightcap Letters;' and the little darlings shall have them
all to themselves."

"Oh, yes! yes! yes! that will be a grand
plan!" cried the children. "Did you ever
hear of such a sensible Aunt Fanny? She
makes it just as we like it."

"If you like this plan," Aunt Fanny goes
on to say, "then the 'Big Nightcap Letters'
are finished with this story sent to Johnny;
and that you will all grow wiser, and better,
and fatter over them, is the loving wish of
your

"AUNT FANNY."

And so the Big Nightcap Letters were ended; and the children went off to bed good,

thankful, and content, and rose the next day good, thankful, and content.

Pray Heaven, dear little reader, you may always do the same.

THE END.